My name is Pisces

(Friends)

Story and art By Lawrence J. King

Friendship is the hardest thing in the world to explain. It's not something you learn in school. But if you haven't learned the meaning of friendship, you haven't learned anything

-Muhammad Ali

This book is dedicated to children, with light hearts, wide smiles, sparkle eyes, hope and prayers for people coming together in harmony.

Thanks to **Theresa Ann Stephens** for her support with my books.

3

Friends

Hello, my name is Pisces; I want to tell you a story about a time when my friends and I had to rethink about what friendship should be.

Once there were four girl friends that lived in a small neighborhood, in a town called Colmar, near our Capitol City, but this could happen in any town or city. We were very happy together and loved school, fun, playing games and spending a lot of time together. My friends' names were Allison, Brianna, Carrie and me, my name is Pisces, yes, my name does not fit Allison, Brianna, or Carrie's in the A, B and C's of name order, so you might say I was a bit different, but really we were as one big, but little friendly girl foursome. We got along just fine, we thought we did and liked all of the same things, even if we dress, wore our hair or looked and sounded a little different. We thought of us as being the same friendly girls with the same likes and dislikes in mostly everything we did, even if that was really impossible. We thought we were best friends for life and that is a very good feeling to have.

One day a new girl was admitted to our school and was seated next to me in my third grade class, over time we slowly began to become friends. One day she shared with me some of her likes and dislikes and that she lives only around the corner from me. We began to become friends with each other. I could see her house from our back window. We later exchange phone numbers, then we texted some with our parent's permission and girl talk sometimes after our home work was done. I liked my new classmate and I plan to introduce her to Allison, Brianna and Carrie, so we could have another friend. I was very excited to have her join us.

Sometimes things do not go as well as planned, I was not so happy anymore, as a matter fact I was in tears as I laid in my bed at night. A day after introducing my new classmate, Debbie to Allison, Brianna and Carrie, I found out that they did not like her as much as I did. Allison was especially outspoken, and said she spoke for Brianna and Carrie in not wanting to be friends with Debbie. She said, "We all think she is not like us at all, we are the same in what we do and the way we all think, I said, "you don't know her that well to know she's not like us" wait until you get to know her better!, But Brianna and Carrie follow Allison as they turned and walked away, not giving me time to explain more things, than Allison turned and said, "forget her if you want to remain friends with us." My head felt to my chest, I thought how bad it would be to lose my friends to gain a new friend, but then again why not be able to gain a new friend to join my current friends.

I wanted to remain friends with Allison, Brianna, and Carrie, so I was sad at the thought of not having them as my friends. I thought about it, why were they being so unwelcoming to Debbie and Debbie did not even know how my friends were feeling about her. She was as nice to them as she had been to me. I was puzzled. And what about my introduction, did I overdo it? Was I too overly excited? Did I take for granted because I liked Debbie my friends would have to like her too? What was it they did not like about her?

Allison felt for the new girl, but deep inside knew Debbie might come in between their foursome. After all she felt five being an odd number would not fit in with their pairing up together as they had for so long. She thought to herself, we did things in twos or all four of us together. If one could not make it to something, either two of us would and two of us would not, so no one would be totally alone. Five was just not going to work; it would not fit into our foursome she thought and she felt Pisces was being a little too quick to ask another girl into their friendship.

The next couple of days my three friends avoided me and Debbie. I had to make a decision, but I was not likening the choice of picking amongst who would be my friend. They all were good friends but now I wonder why they were turning into unfriendly girls, just because they thought Debbie would not fit in with us. I would not bring a bad girl into our friendship. Debbie and I were alike in some ways-- no one is all the same, I thought. I did not know what to do, what would you do? Allison was leading our friends to believe my new friend should not be friends with all of us. We had a problem, and my friends were not seeing eye to eye with me over Debbie. Unfriendly gossip was taking the lead in ruining our special friendship, and that's not a good thing, something had to be done before we grew too far apart.

Brianna thought Debbie would not fit in with us either, she felt she looked and acted too shy when I introduced her and she was so tall, she just did not look like she would fit in with us. Carrie had laugh when Debbie began to talk, she later spread talk that Debbie's voice sounded funny to her and that she dress in funny looking colors.

You are supposed to hold onto good friends, friends don't come easy or often. Good friends are close almost like family, so I thought. Well maybe we are not all thinking on the same level; maybe we need a break, a time out, to think what friends are really about and what they should not be about. Can friends be only people who do the same things you do? Or can they do different things as long as it does not hurt other people. I was not entirely like Allison, Brianna, Carrie or Debbie. Or now maybe the new A, B, C, or D, I'm Pisces, but I don't want to be an island, I do want to have friends, in my life. Would Debbie be one of them or will I keep Allison, Brianna, and Carrie. I really don't want to be on a lonely island without friends that would be really sad to me.

Pisces made her decision, when in real doubt, seek experienced help, so she went for guidance, to those who know about friends, elderly friends, young friends, new friends, old friends, past and present friends, they even know something about her friends, now they would help Pisces to add or subtract to her list of friends. It's good to have wisdom close by and she planned to use it for the good of all of her friends. Pisces cross her fingers behind her back, she listen, and took in what was being said and she put in her penny's worth too, asking questions and listening with all her attention to the subject at hand. In the end Pisces was so happy to have asked her parents for advice. After all was said and done, Pisces had renewed confidence in being honest with her friends to explain in the best way she could to try to bring good friends with some differences together and of course Pisces would listen to what Allison, Brianna and Carrie had to say too.

Not liking someone or not giving them a chance in friendship because of small differences may not be right. How will Allison and the girls feel when I speak from my heart, will my words to their ears make any difference in their choice of our friendship. I hope for a long and continued friendship; the doubt in my mind had left. Tomorrow I start at the beginning, where it all began to bring some good reasoning in putting our dislikes to rest.

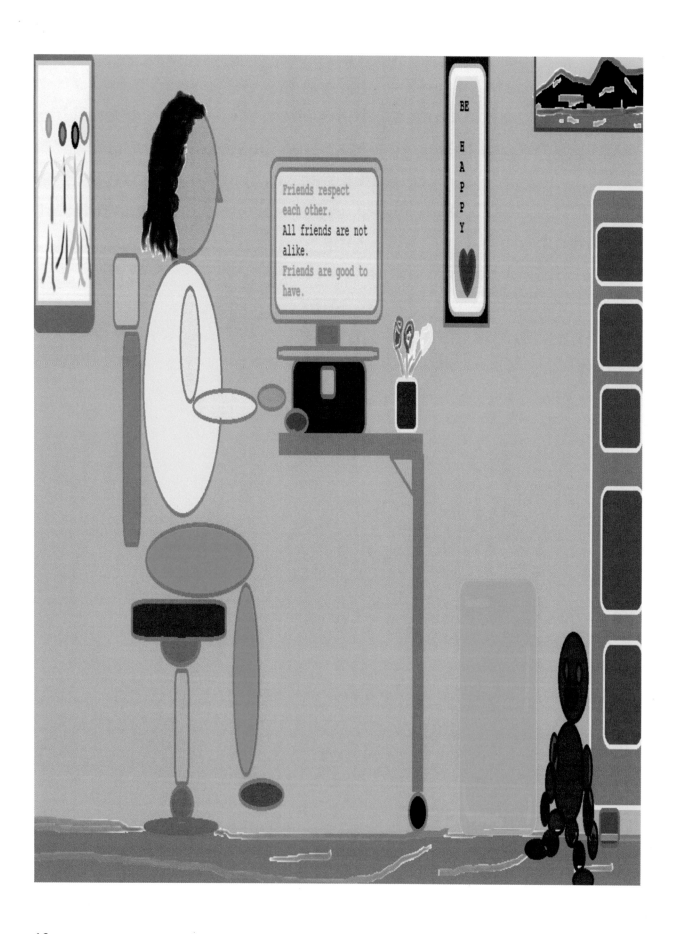

The next day when I saw my three friends, I quickly walked up to them and said hello. They all spoke. Then I looked at Allison who had been leading the pack to not let Debbie come into our friendship. I said, "I want all of us friends to remain friends, I hope you all understand how friends can remain or become friends who may not be alike in some ways. I want to tell you, Brianna and Carrie about Debbie, maybe I was a little too excited in my first introduction." They all gathered in closely to hear my soft- spoken words. I did not want to stop talking until I completed all my thoughts, so I continued, "Debbie and I are both the same age, like Brianna and I are. Debbie and are alike, we enjoy funny movies like we all do, we laugh a lot like we all do, and we like to eat pizzas, listen to pop music, and chill with ice cream." Brianna and Carrie nodded their heads in agreement.

"Debbie and I are different too." Allison nodded her head in agreement. " She likes olives on her pizza. I like lots of green peppers on mine. Debbie like guitar sounds the most, I like saxophone sounds the most, she likes French vanilla ice cream best, I like butter pecan ice cream.

18

We all love to savory the pleasant smell of fresh flowers, we all smell them when we can, we like ripen fruit trees and colorful summer bugs on those hot lazy days of summer." "Debbie and I are different, she likes carnations flowers, I like tulips, she likes apple trees with big green apples, I like juicy peach trees, she likes lighting bugs and I like colorful lady bugs." "Me too!" Carrie said with a snicker of a laugh.

"We all like interesting jobs. Debbie says she would like to be a doctor when she grows up, I like nursing. We all like the circus when it comes to town. Debbie likes seeing the clowns just like you and Carrie always do." Allison let a small smile cross her lips as her interest grew. Brianna and I liked tightrope walkers the best when we went to the circus the last time. Carrie liked the elephants and Brianna favors those beautiful Arabian horses. I think we all do, we all have our likes and differences."

Brianna asked, "Does she like to jump double Dutch?"
"Does she like cats like I do?" asked Allison. Pisces continued, "We both like who we are, she likes being taller, just like you do Allison, her hair is straight like Carrie's and mine is curly like yours and Brianna. We are alike, we are different-- friends should be fair and honest with each other. I hope we can all be friends with our small differences."

Carrie and Brianna exchange happy looks and Allison took a deep breath and threw both of her arms to the sky in a joyous way. Then Allison said, "Yes, we are different! Your likes and differences are different then mind sometimes but we get along! I was wrong speaking only about our differences when we have so many things in common and maybe I judge Debbie too quickly, not wanting our friendship to get out of control." Allison reached her arms out and hugged Pisces, her wide toothy grin returned as Brianna and Carrie join in the hugging. Pisces was so happy and a little surprise at how well Allison, Brianna and Carrie had been so open to her words. Pisces said, "I wished I would have told you all more about Debbie before I introduce her maybe I was just too excited. Allison said, "I apologize for all of the negative gossip I started." Brianna and Carrie, said "we share some blame too, we missed being friendly with you." Carrie said, "It was impolite for me to laugh at how I thought Debbie sounded too, I felt bad afterwards, and I want to let Debbie know I'm sorry for that."

We are different, I like me for who I am, and I like my friends for who they are, we are a like in ways and different in ways, we can be friends with our small differences and learn to respect each other more. Now we are all happy, Allison, Brianna, Carrie, Debbie and I are all friends.

My name is Pisces; maybe you are our new friend.

Be slow to fall into friendship, but when you are in, continue firm and constant.

-Socrates

The end

Lawrence is a life-long resident of Washington, DC; married and the father of four sons. He is a graduate of the 1967 class of Cardozo High School and he enjoys real life stories, sports, music, family and friends. He is also the author of Crumbs (Cousins, Relatives, Uncles, Mothers, Brothers, Sisters) a story of Julie, her life and struggles raising her three youngest children in the Nation's Capital. This is his second children book. His first children's book is titled "A Mom and Me Day!"

Thank you for your support of my books. More books are plan in the near future.

Made in the USA
Middletown, DE
28 October 2020